STevie's
TRICYCLe

by Pnina Moed-Kass
illustrated by Lorna Tomei

A GOLDEN BOOK, New York
Western Publishing Company, Inc., Racine, Wisconsin 53404

It's bedtime now.

Stevie puts his tricycle in its special place.

Tomorrow Stevie will ride
his tricycle again.

And he never leaves it out in the rain.

Stevie takes good care of his tricycle.
He shines the handlebars and polishes
the bell every day.

And sometimes he pretends he's sailing a big boat.

Sometimes, when Stevie rides his tricycle,
he pretends he's driving a fire engine.

Now Stevie can give Teddy a ride in the yard.

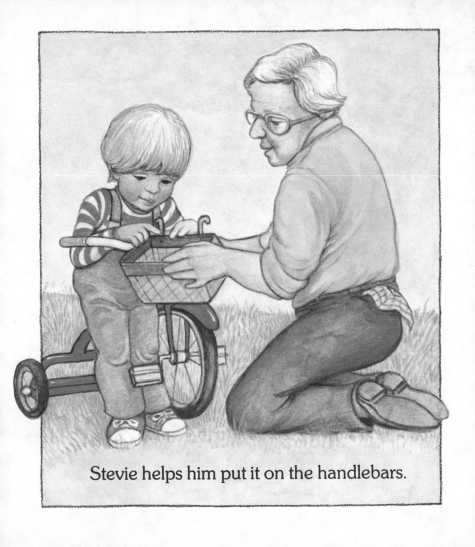

Stevie helps him put it on the handlebars.

Grandpa has a basket for Stevie's tricycle.

The cat knows he's coming, too.

When Stevie rings his bell,
people know he's coming.

He can go next door to Betsy's house.

he can go in a squiggly line.

When Stevie's legs go around and around,
the pedals turn. That makes the tricycle go.
Stevie can go in a straight line, or . . .

Here is Stevie sitting on his tricycle.
His hands are on the handlebars.
His feet are on the pedals.

Stevie's tricycle has three wheels.
It has two pedals.
It has a seat.
It has handlebars.
It even has a bell!

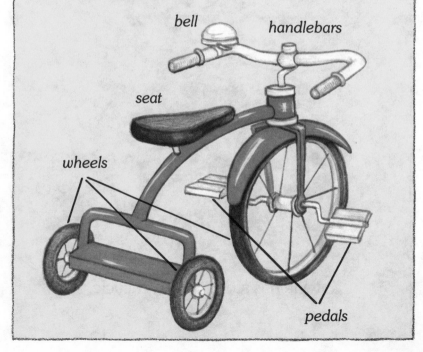

bell

handlebars

seat

wheels

pedals

Stevie has a brand-new tricycle.